DINOSAURS Don't DRAW

For Maggie and Robert,
who know far more about art than I ever will – E.W.

For the inspirational and hilarious Rita Seyben-Geven – S.L.

First published 2018 by Macmillan Children's Books,
an imprint of Pan Macmillan, 20 New Wharf Road, London N1 9RR.
Associated companies throughout the world.
www.panmacmillan.com

ISBN: 978-1-4472-5482-9 (HB)
ISBN:978-1-4472-5483-6 (PB)

1 3 5 7 9 8 6 4 2

Printed in China

DINOSAURS
Don't
DRAW

Written by
Elli Woollard

Illustrated by
Steven Lenton

MACMILLAN CHILDREN'S BOOKS

One morning as Picassaur wandered around
He found something small, rather strange, on the ground.

What could it be? It was making a trail
As magic as moonlight and silvery pale.

Picassaur looked and, "I wonder . . ." he said,
With a swish of his tail and a flick of his head.
"Maybe . . ." he said, and he lifted a claw.
He clutched at the white thing and started to draw.

Then out of the white thing came mountains as high
As the whispery winds and the stars in the sky.

And Picassaur gazed, quite amazed, and said, "Wow!
I must show my mother! I'll show her right now."

"What have you got?"
said his mum with a frown.
"Let go of that white thing!
Come on, put it down!

"Dinosaurs gnash and dinosaurs bash.

They **splash**
and they **dash**

and they **smash**
and they **crash**.

"They nibble and dribble, they nip and they gnaw,
But whatever they do, they do not ever draw.
We're fighters, we're biters, as fierce as can be!
Come to the forest and then you will see."

But down at the lake was some beautiful ooze,
And Picassaur said, "Let me see . . . what to choose?"
Out of those colours came flashes as frightening
As fiery volcanoes and lashes of lightning.

And Picassaur stared, rather scared, and said, "Wow!
I must show my father! I'll show him right now."

"Oh, Picassaur, Picassaur,
what's all this mess?
Your mother and I
are in dreadful distress!

"Dinosaurs chomp and dinosaurs clomp.

They **stamp**
and they **stomp**

and they **romp**
in the swamp.

"They nibble and dribble, they nip and they gnaw,
But whatever they do, they do not ever draw.
We're brave and we're bold; we're as fierce as can be!
Come to the forest and then you will see."

But down by the woods were some sticks, old and charred.
And Picassaur thought, and he wondered quite hard.
Then out of that black stuff came clouds all aglow
With a bittersweet winter and glitter of snow.

And Picassaur shook as he looked and said, "Wow!
I must show my cousins! I'll show them right now!"

But down at the forest they yelled, "Come and fight!
Forget all your drawing - there's battle tonight.

"Dinosaurs prowl and dinosaurs scowl.

We howl
and we growl

and our tempers
are foul."

And they ran and they rolled in the muck and the mud.
But then, from the forest, they heard a loud . . .

THUD!

And there stood a T-rex
as tall as ten trees,
With his eyes flaming fire,
while his breath boiled the breeze.
The dinosaurs quaked.
The dinosaurs quivered.

They yelped out for **help**
and they shook
and they shivered.

The T-rex yelled, "Yum!" and he lifted his jaw.
But then he whipped round and he gaped as he saw . . .

A fearsome foul dino, whose jaws were so wide
They would easily fit a whole T-rex inside!
"Aaaargh!" wailed the T-rex and raced down the track
Till he reached the far mountains, and didn't come back!

Then Picassaur's family said, "Hip hip hooray!
Three cheers for our artist! Our son's saved the day!
Picassaur, sorry, we got it all wrong.
Dinosaurs DO draw - you knew all along."

And everyone said, "Let us try something new."
So they picked up some chalk and the dinosaurs . . .